Fox Friend

by

Michael Morpurgo

Illustrated by Joanna Carey

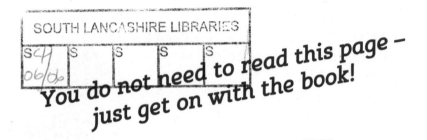
First published in 2006 in Great Britain by
Barrington Stoke Ltd

This edition based on *Fox Friend*, published by
Barrington Stoke in 2005

ISBN 1-842994-10-7
13 digit ISBN 978-1-84299-410-8

Printed in Great Britain by Bell & Bain Ltd

Meet The Author – Michael Morpurgo

What is your favourite animal?
Elephant
What is your favourite boy's name?
George
What is your favourite girl's name?
Eleanor
What is your favourite food?
Prawns
What is your favourite music?
"Spem in Alium"
by Thomas Tallis
What is your favourite hobby?
Writing

Meet The Illustrator – Joanna Carey

What is your favourite animal?
My cat, Alfie
What is your favourite boy's name?
I have three favourites – Joseph, Felix
and Daniel
What is your favourite girl's name?
Amy
What is your favourite food?
Smoked salmon
What is your favourite music?
Bach piano music
What is your favourite hobby?
Making things out of things

To dear Lindsey and Kathryn,
fellow musketeers on our
great adventure

Contents

Chapter 1
Farm Life

Clare had lived all her life on the farm, but she'd never seen a fox. She was 12 now. You can live a very long time on a farm and not see a fox. You will see one more often in a town garden or a city street.

Clare's dad and mum had a farm which was close to the moors in Devon. They kept sheep, over 300 of them.

Summer and winter, the sheep were out on the steep hills around the farm-house. There were three cows and a few hens and geese as well. And Clare had her own horse, Red. She liked to ride him as often as she could. Red was her best friend. Clare was happy when she could gallop out over the moors on Red, or groom him in his stable. Clare spent a lot of time in there. She liked to talk to him. Clare was an only child. But she had Red, and that was all she wanted.

Clare saw her first fox on the way back from school one day. It was just a bit of good luck. It was cold and it was getting dark when Clare saw the fox. He came trotting out into the road right in front of her. He didn't seem at all scared. He lifted his nose and sniffed the air. Then he ran across the road in front of Clare, jumped up onto the grass bank and was gone.

"He was really lovely," she said at supper.

"Lovely? Foxes aren't lovely, Clare," her dad said. He was looking very angry. "The only good fox is a dead fox. We've lost ten lambs this year. Foxes ate them all. And two hens just last week. Foxes are killers. That's what they are, killers."

"They've got to eat," Clare said. She was getting angry now, too.

"Clare only meant that they *look* lovely," said her mum. Clare and her dad were always at war. Her mum tried to stop them. But it was very hard.

"A tiger looks lovely," Clare's dad went on. "But he's still a killer. That lovely fox you saw may be the one that killed my

4

lambs. Anyway with a bit of luck it won't be around much longer."

"What do you mean?" asked Clare.

"The fox hunt. They're coming tomorrow. They'll be hunting all over the moor. The hounds will soon sniff him out, and that'll be the end of him."

"Well I think hunting foxes is cruel," said Clare. "All those horses and hounds chasing after one poor little fox. It's cruel."

"But you have to hunt foxes, Clare," her mum said. "If you didn't there would be too many of them."

"There's too many of us," Clare snapped back, "but no-one goes around hunting us, do they? It's not right and it's not fair."

5

"Maybe it isn't fair," her father said. "But that's how it is. One thing you've got to learn, Clare," he went on, "is that life isn't fair. You want it to be. We all do. But it isn't."

Chapter 2
The Rescue

Later that night when Clare groomed Red she told him all about the fox she'd seen and about the hunt. She always told him everything.

It was March and new lambs were being born every day. Clare's father and mother had to check all the time to see that all was well. Sometimes the sheep needed help. Sometimes the lambs were weak. Clare

helped at week-ends, and sometimes after school. She liked doing it. She would ride out on Red. Some of the sheep were in fields far away from the farm-house. Clare loved the lambs.

The next day was Saturday. When Clare woke up all she could think of was the fox she had seen in the road. The hunt would be coming after him today.

Her Dad had fetched all the sheep back into the barns before breakfast. It was going to snow, he said. He didn't want them out in the snow. He asked Clare to go up onto the moor and have a last look. He had to be sure he hadn't missed any sheep up there.

So after breakfast, Clare rode off to look for any lost sheep. As she rode over the hills she could hear the hunting horn and the yelping of the fox hounds. The hunt had

begun. She could see now that the horses had been this way. There were hoof prints everywhere. She was up on the high hill behind the farm now. From here she could see over all the fields. But there were no lost lambs. The sky was very grey. There would be snow soon.

She was coming back down the hill when she saw Red's ears prick up. He'd heard something. Then *she* heard it too. Something was moving in the tall grass beside the path. She stopped. For a moment she could hear only the wind. But Red's ears still twitched. He gave a snort. He was a bit scared. Then out of the tall grass came a small fox cub. He was so weak he could hardly walk. His coat wasn't red brown like grown-up foxes. It was grey brown, and very wet. His tail hung down like a bit of wet rope. And his left ear had been torn. There was blood on the side of his face, and

all down his neck. Somehow, he must have got away from the hounds. He looked up at Clare out of big wide eyes.

Clare jumped off Red and bent down. She held out her hand to the fox cub, very slowly. She did not want to scare him. "Hello," she said, "you're a brave little fox. They can't do anything bad to you now. I won't let them. I'm not like them. I don't want to kill you. I want to look after you."

The fox cub was too weak to run away. He yelped at her and snarled a little when she stroked him. But he didn't bite. He didn't struggle much when she picked him up. Clare tucked him inside her coat to keep him warm. She showed him to Red who snorted again and shook his head. "You don't need to be scared, Red," she said. "It's just a fox cub."

Clare didn't get back up on Red. He walked behind her. And as they went Clare told Red about her plans. "I've got a good place to hide the cub," she said. "I can only tell you, Red. If I tell Dad, I know he'd kill him. If I tell Mum, she'll tell Dad. So it's our secret, Red, yours and mine.

There's only one place I can think of. The old fishing hut down by the river. You know, the place where I made my den last summer. No-one goes there but me. I'll keep him there. He can yelp and yap as much as he likes and no-one will hear him. It's miles away from the house. He'll be safe there. I can feed him in there and keep him warm and look after him. He'll be fine. No-one will ever find out, will they? Not if I'm careful."

Chapter 3
The Orphan

When they got to the fishing hut, Clare looked around to make sure no-one was around to see them. The door was a bit stiff. She had to kick it open. It was dark inside. But at least it was dry. There were some old sacks in the corner. She knelt down and put the fox cub down on them.

She said to him, "I know it's not very cosy. But you'll be warm in here, and dry. You'll be fine." The cub lay down in the corner. He was looking at her as she spoke. And he was shaking. "I'll clean up that ear of yours," Clare went on, "and you'll need food too. Milk, lots of it. You look as if you're starving. I've got to go now. But I'll be right back."

So she left the fox cub safe in the fishing hut, and rode Red back home. It was not hard to find some milk for the cub. At this time of year there were always lambs that had to be fed by hand, out of a bottle. *What is good for a lamb,* Clare thought, *is good for a fox cub.* She mixed the milk powder with warm water. Not too hot. Not too cold. Just then her mum came into the kitchen.

"I need this for one of the lambs that's lost its mum," Clare said, rushing past her

mother. "I've got to hurry. Can't stop, Mum. See you."

She rode Red at a gallop all the way back down to the river. She was holding on tight to the bottle with one hand. When she got there the fox cub was yapping inside the fishing hut.

But when she tried to feed him, he pulled away.

He didn't seem to know what to do. He got more milk on his nose than in his mouth. He snapped at Clare. He even tried to bite her. But then he licked his nose to clean it and tasted the milk. He licked again. He liked it. He wanted more. So Clare dropped some more milk on his nose. He licked it off. Clare pressed the teat of the bottle against his mouth. The mouth opened and at last he began to suck. NOW he had the idea. NOW he could do it. He sucked hard but he still wasn't very good at it. There was milk all over his face. Soon the milk had all gone.

Now Clare cleaned up his torn ear. Half of it was missing. She washed it very gently. All the time she was talking to the fox cub. He let her clean his ear. And all the time he looked up into her eyes.

"I'll get you better," Clare told him. "I'll bring you milk as often as I can. I'll make you well again. I'll come back tomorrow. I can't come too often, or they'll find out about you. I'll think of a name for you and get you some more milk."

The fox cub sat on the pile of old sacks and licked his lips. He looked as if he knew what she was saying.

Chapter 4
Larry

Clare could hardly eat her supper. She kept thinking about the fox cub down in the fishing hut. She kept hoping he was all right.

"You're not eating," said her mum. "Is something the matter?"

"No," Clare said. Her dad came in. He shook the snow off his boots. "It's a good

thing we fetched the sheep in off the hills," he said. "The snow-storm's bad out there."

All night the snow fell and the wind howled around the farm-house. But that wasn't why Clare lay awake. She was looking out of her window at the falling snow. It was blowing across the farm-yard. It was piling up against the barn. And all the time she could think of nothing but the fox cub. Was he warm in the hut? Had he all the milk he needed? Would he still be alive in the morning? She was thinking about him for ages. But at last she was so tired she fell asleep.

Clare came down early the next morning. The snow had stopped.

Everywhere was white and silent. Her mum was up and cooking breakfast.

"I've got to feed that lamb," Clare told her. "He'll be cold and hungry." She made up the bottle as fast as she could, then put on her coat and boots.

"What about your breakfast?" her mum called after Clare as she ran out.

"Later, Mum," said Clare. And then she was gone.

She took Red. Clare knew she'd get there faster on Red. And she knew how much Red loved the snow. So she got him ready and rode over the fields to the fishing hut. The milk was safe inside her coat.

She had to brush away the snow before she could open the door of the hut. How pleased the fox cub was to see her! And how pleased she was to see him! He didn't mind at all when she picked him up.

"Larry," said Clare. "Larry, that's what I'll call you. You're my orphan lamb, Larry. You may look a bit foxy. You may have pointy ears, well, one pointy ear. You may have a bushy tail. But you're a lamb, do you hear? You'll have to learn to baa like a proper sheep."

The torn ear had not bled any more. "Your ear looks fine," she said. "Why do little foxes have such big ears? Maybe they won't look so big when you're a grown-up fox, when the rest of you is bigger. And just now you're hungry, aren't you?"

Larry's nose was trying to find the bottle. This time he knew what to do. He sucked hard, until the milk was all gone. Even then he wanted to go on sucking. Clare sat down on his sacks. At once Larry jumped up onto her lap. Clare could feel he was very thin.

"I'd like to keep you always, but I can't," she said as she stroked him on the top of his head. His fur was so soft. "What am I going to do with you, Larry?" But Larry said nothing. He was too busy licking himself.

Chapter 5
Growing Up

For the next few weeks Clare fed Larry every day. Sometimes, as he grew bigger, she fed him twice a day. He was always hungry. No-one found out about him. And she told no-one, not even her best friend at school. She had told Red, but then she told Red all her secrets. But he wasn't much help to her.

"Shall I let him go now, Red?" she asked him again and again. "Would he be OK on his own yet, Red?"

Red would just snort and toss his head.

Larry's ear was better now. He was fatter and his fur shone. He wanted to play all the time. He'd loved ripping his sacks to bits. Clare and he would play together for hours in the dark hut. She didn't dare take him out, in case someone saw, in case he ran off.

Winter was over now and it was the spring holidays. Clare was so happy. She could go and see Larry even more often. And she had to, because he was getting more and more hungry. But her mum and dad had begun to ask her where she went off to all the time. Most of all when she'd been out all day.

"Where do you get to?" her mum asked.

"Just out riding," Clare told her. "Red needs to get out."

"Just riding?" She knew her mum didn't believe her.

"And I watch birds," Clare said. "You have to hang around for ages if you want to see them."

"What sort of birds?" her dad asked.

"All sorts, ducks, robins, tits ..." She saw her mum and dad look at each another. They still didn't believe her. She could feel it. She knew that sooner or later they were going to find out. One of them would see her coming out of the fishing hut. Or they would follow her down there. She hadn't got much time.

Clare knew Larry would be OK on his own now. For some time now she'd been giving him less and less milk and more meat. He loved it. Larry was no longer a cub. He was growing into a fox. His nose was more pointed. His coat had lost its grey. He was big and brown now. His tail was long and bushy. Larry would soon be a grown-up fox.

Each time Clare came with his food and each time she left him, he would scratch at the door of the fishing hut. He wanted to get out. He'd yelp and bark and moan too. And loud, too loud.

Someone was going to hear him. But, in the end, that wasn't why Clare let him go.

Chapter 6
Decision Time

One morning she was riding away from the fishing hut on Red. She could hear Larry, scratching at the door and yelping.

"It's not right, is it, Red?" Clare said. "He wants to be free. He wants to be wild again. The fishing hut has become a prison. I've got to let him go." She had made up her mind.

She let him go that afternoon. She took a fresh sack with her and rode down to the fishing hut. She fed him for the last time, put him in the sack and carried him out of the hut. It was dark in the sack and Larry lay still. Clare talked to him all the time, as she got up on Red and rode away, up onto the high moor. Her plan was to ride as far away as she could. Then she'd let him go on the moor and just let him try to look after himself. She hoped he could hunt for himself now. *He could eat worms*, she thought. *He could catch mice and even rabbits.*

She came to a place in a rocky valley full of trees. It was out of the wind and there was a stream to drink from. There were rabbit holes all around, too. *This will be a good place for Larry*, she thought.

Red drank from the stream as she got Larry out of the sack. He stood there looking about him, sniffing the air.

"Off you go, Larry," said Clare. "Go on. Go away. Please."

She was crying. She couldn't help it. Larry sat down and looked up at her. His good ear twitched.

"I have to leave you, don't you see?" Clare said. "I don't want to, but I have to. You've got to be a fox now, not a pet. Go off now."

But he wouldn't. In the end she just left him. As she rode off she didn't look back. She knew that if she'd seen him still sitting there, she'd want to go back, pick him up and take him home. She rode hard all the way back to the farm. She just hoped she'd done the right thing.

All night long she lay awake thinking about Larry. She was up as soon as it was light. She had to know, to find out if he was all right. She rode to the wood, to the spot where she'd left him. He wasn't there. She called for him again and again. He did not come. Clare rode all the way down the valley beside the stream. He wasn't there. Was she sad or happy? She was both. She was sad he was gone, but happy he wasn't out there, just sitting and waiting for her to come back.

"Be happy, Larry," she called out. "Be happy!" And she rode home.

Chapter 7
Tragedy

The next day Clare helped her mum clean out the sheep pens in the barn. It was mucky work, but it made her feel good. They had just got to the end when a gunshot rang out across the farm-yard.

They ran out of the barn. Clare's dad was standing by the hen house. He had a gun. "Just look at that?" he said. At his feet lay a dead fox. "And in the daytime, too. I

saw him walking towards the hen house just as if he belonged here."

"Did he kill any hens?" Clare's mum asked.

"I don't think so," said her father. He bent down over the dead fox. "I got him before he got them. Looks like a young one. He's had half his ear torn off somehow." Her father was looking at Clare now. "Nothing to be sad about, Clare. Like I told you. The only good fox is a dead fox."

A Letter from the Author

Dear Reader,

I live on a farm in Devon. Even so, I don't see foxes very often. They're shy animals, and keep clear of human beings if they can. But I do see them sometimes. I saw one once running off across the field with a chicken in its mouth. I saw another tucked up in the long grass on the top of a bank. I thought he was asleep, but he wasn't. He was dead.

I hear them barking sometimes at night. And sometimes the hunt comes down our lane. Once a fox hound got lost and ended up in our garden. She went to sleep in our shed. Was she dreaming of foxes?

In my mind *Fox Friend* happens on our farm. I could just see it all as I wrote it. I hope you can see it too as you read it. I hope you love reading it as much as I loved writing it.

****

Maybe I should tell you a bit about the farm where I live.

Most farms have cows or sheep or pigs or hens or geese or ducks. Our farm does too. But our farm has children too, 1,000 of them every year. (Not all at once!) They don't come just for a walk round. They come for a whole week to help run the farm. They are the farm workers! Just so long as it's safe, the children do it. (They don't go into the field with a bull, for example!)

And it's a *real* farm, not a play farm where you come to cuddle a lamb and stroke a horse, though they do that too.

It's a huge farm too. It's about as big as 250 football pitches. There are 80 milking cows, 500 sheep, 40 pigs, 100 beef cattle, 50 calves, 35 ducks, 42 hens, 3 geese, 3 donkeys, a horse and a whole lot of farm cats and dogs.

The teachers and children who come here stay for a week.

There's a playroom (we call it the "noisy room") with ping-pong and table football. There's a classroom and a sitting room with lots of books.

Outside there's a big field to run around in, with cow-pats for goal posts. Nice and messy!

****

This is what the children do every day.

7 am: Get up. Have a cup of tea. Go out on the farm in three groups (12 in each). One group goes to milk the cows. Another goes to feed the pigs and calves. Another

feeds the horse and donkeys, and opens up the hens and ducks and geese. Back for breakfast.

9.30 am: Out onto the farm again, one group brushes down the dairy. Another feeds or moves the sheep. Another puts the horse and donkeys out. Another cleans out the stables and feeds the hens and ducks and geese.

11 am: Time for a break and a drink and a biscuit. (We need it!)

After our break, it's work in the classroom, or it's playtime.

After lunch, we go out to work on the farm again in our three groups. What we do depends on the time of year and the weather.

We clean out sheds (lots of these), bring
in logs for the fires, pick up apples and
potatoes (at harvest time), pick raspberries,
strawberries in the walled garden or look
for blackberries in the hedges. We help with

the corn harvest. There is always something that needs to be done.

We have three good, hot meals a day. (I don't do the cooking, which is lucky for the children!) Supper is at 5 pm. Then at 6 pm off we go again.

The groups change jobs so everyone gets a turn. The cows have to be milked, the pigs and calves have to be fed, the horse and donkeys have to be fetched in from the field. The eggs must be collected and the hens and ducks and geese have to be shut up for the night, in case the fox comes. And he does come all too often.

We come back to the house at 7.30 pm for a hot chocolate and a story. I go up once a week to read them a story. And one of the ones I like best is *Fox Friend*.

If you or your teacher or your mum or dad would like to know more about the farm visits – we call it Farms for City Children – then you can write to me, Michael Morpurgo, at:

Nethercott House
Iddesleigh
Winkleigh
Devon
EX9 8BG

Farms for City Children is a charity with three such farms – one in Wales, one in Gloucestershire and one here in Devon. We now welcome over 3,000 primary school children from our towns and cities ever year.

Maybe your school would like to come too. I hope so.

All the best,

Michael Morpurgo

If you loved this story, why don't you read ...

Who's A Big Bully Then?

by Michael Morpurgo

How would you feel if you beat the school bully in a race? And then he wanted a fight? What would you do? Find out what happens to Darren in front of all his friends.

4u2read.ok!